GIGANTOSAURUS™

Rock Out, ROCKY

CANDLEWICK
ENTERTAINMENT

First U.S. edition 2020
First published by Templar Books, an imprint of Bonnier Books UK 2020

Library of Congress Catalog Card Number pending
ISBN 978-1-5362-1408-6

20 21 22 23 24 25 TWP 10 9 8 7 6 5 4 3 2 1

Printed in Johor Bahru, Malaysia

This book was typeset in Kosmik BoldOne and Kosmik PlainTwo.
The illustrations were created digitally.

Candlewick Entertainment
an imprint of
Candlewick Press
99 Dover Street
Somerville, Massachusetts 02144

visit us at www.candlewick.com

Rocky has hidden **ten** of his favorite Giganto cards throughout this book.

Can you find them all?

This story is all about **ROCKY**, the plucky parasaurolophus. He's the fastest, strongest, and TOUGHEST dino in all of Cretacea . . . or so he thinks! Here's how Rocky learned that sometimes even the toughest dinosaur needs a little help from his friends!

It was a sunny day in the jungle and Rocky had challenged himself to complete another daring mission.

This time, he was running as fast as he could up the fiery path of the biggest volcano in the land—MOUNT OBLIVION!

"How am I doing?" Rocky called to his friends.

"You're on track to break the record!" shouted Mazu as she timed him on her sundial rock.

Fastest climb to the top of Mount Oblivion!

Rocky cheered proudly and paused to deliver a speech.

"That's me—ROCKY. The TOUGHEST, FASTEST volcano climber in all the land. Soon every dinosaur will know who I am."

Even **GIGANTOSAURUS!**

Mazu, Bill, and Tiny had heard this speech before.

"He's daydreaming about his hero again," they said.

As Rocky stepped back, he tripped over a small rock and sent it flying. He was a very daring dinosaur, but also VERY clumsy.

The small rock bumped into a HUGE boulder, which went rolling down the volcano fast—straight toward his friends!

Luckily the boulder missed the other dinos by an inch. But poor Rocky had hurt his foot on the rock. His friends rushed over to take care of him.

Rocky pulled out his trusty
Giganto cards and held them up
one by one to prove his point.

"See—here he is jogging . . . ALONE.

And here he is in a mud bath
built for ONE!

"And my personal favorite—here's Giganto food shopping," he said.
"ALONE. So I, too, have to prove how tough I am. ALONE."

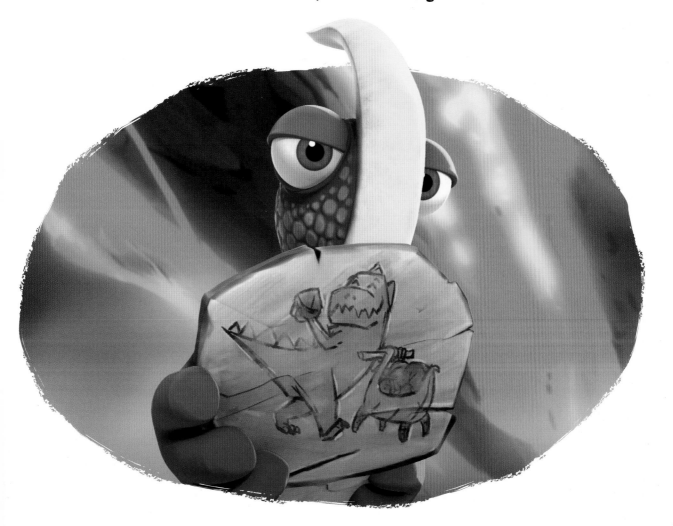

Rocky's friends sighed. How would Rocky make it to the top of the volcano
with a sore toe if he wouldn't let them help?

Suddenly, the ground underneath the dinos SHOOK with a mighty RUMBLE. It was a GROUNDWOBBLER!

The cliff the little dinosaurs were standing on broke away from the mountain with a CRACK and took them sailing down the river of lava at full speed! At the base of the volcano they slid to a sudden stop and Rocky soared through the air . . .

before landing neatly in Tiny's arms.

Gotcha, tough guy!

"Ugh, Tiny, why did you have to help me?" asked Rocky. "I told you, I don't need ANYONE'S help!"

The groundwobbler noise was coming from the trees—and it was getting much louder! As the friends stopped to listen, a stampede of dinosaurs rushed past them, fleeing the sound.

That gave Rocky an idea.

"I'm going to check it out," he said. "If I can't get to the top of Mount Oblivion in record time, then I'll stop the earth from wobbling instead!"

"Is your crest filled with coconuts?" asked Bill. "You don't run TOWARD danger—you run AWAY from it!"

"Not this parasora . . . parasloppa . . . SUPER DINO!" said Rocky, heading toward the rumbling sound.

"I think he meant 'parasaurolophus'!" said Mazu.

Rocky was happy to be back on his mission. As he walked along, he was busy thinking up a tough-sounding new nickname for himself. *It needs to be something super cool, like ... GIGANTO,* he thought.

Rockinator? Rockster? ROCKLEDOODLEDOO?

I know just what will help!

The others heard Rocky shout out in pain and hurried over to help. His toe was still hurting badly.

Mazu pointed ahead. "This is a bulb from a java plant," she explained. "It's full of gel that will help your toe feel better."

"I don't NEED your help!" Rocky said angrily. He was still annoyed with his friends for trying to help.

"Everybody needs help sometimes," said Mazu.

But Rocky wouldn't listen. "Not tough guys like . . .

"GIGANTOSAURUS!"

Giganto had appeared in a clearing ahead, roaring and thrashing his tail around. "Wow!" Rocky gazed up at his idol with wonder.

Suddenly, the mighty dinosaur started to hop UP and DOWN on one foot and the ground began to RUMBLE and SHAKE. . . . So Giganto was the groundwobbler! But why was he stomping around so much?

Then Mazu spotted something in Giganto's foot. "Isn't that the boulder Rocky knocked over earlier?" she asked. Sure enough, the same rock was now wedged between Giganto's toes.

Poor Giganto!
He's hurt!

"I bet if we calm him down, we could get that rock out from between his toes," said Tiny.

Rocky sprang into action. It was his fault, so he thought he should be the one to fix it! How could he calm Giganto down? "I've got it!" he said excitedly. "When I was a baby, my mom would MOO to help me relax."

Rocky took a deep breath and blew air out of the crest on his head. It made a deep MOOOOOOO sound that echoed through the jungle. Giganto stopped stomping and tilted his head to listen.

"I think it's working!" said Mazu.

MOOOOOOOOO

"He needs to hear me better. I've got to get closer!" said Rocky.
He scrambled over to a palm tree and started to climb up, up, up!

But he slipped and fell down with a CRASH!
Rocky wasn't going anywhere with that sore foot.

Mazu squirted the gel from the java plant onto Rocky's foot. He instantly felt better! "See how nice a little help can be?" she said.

"I'm sorry," said Rocky, looking up at his friends. "I should have just accepted your help in the first place."

Then the ground shook again, and Rocky remembered his mission.

"Giganto!" he cried. "Now it's HIS turn to feel better. I'm coming, big guy! Uh . . . I mean, WE'RE coming."

That's better!

With his foot feeling much better, Rocky hopped up onto a tree branch and blew air out of his crest to relax the huge dinosaur. Mazu and Tiny used a bamboo stick to pry the rock out from between Giganto's toes. Then Bill spread java gel onto his foot to make it feel better.

You see, even tough guys like us need help!

The four dino friends cheered as Giganto stomped off.
He seemed much happier.

"Rocky, you did it!" said Tiny. "You helped Giganto to feel better!"

"No," said Rocky. "WE did it. I couldn't have done it without you!"

That was how Rocky learned that sometimes the toughest thing a dinosaur can do is accept help from his friends—even when he thinks he doesn't need it! Rocky became a much more humble dinosaur after that. Well, for a few minutes at least!

Wait—this book is all about ME? I'M FAMOUS!

Here he goes again!